# WAY PAST
# BEDTIME

# WAY PAST
# BEDTIME

written by
## TARA LAZAR

illustrated by
## RICH WAKE

ALADDIN
NEW YORK  LONDON  TORONTO  SYDNEY  NEW DELHI

# ALADDIN

An imprint of Simon & Schuster Children's Publishing Division
1230 Avenue of the Americas, New York, New York 10020
First Aladdin hardcover edition April 2017
Text copyright © 2017 by Tara Lazar
Illustrations copyright © 2017 by Rich Wake

For information about special discounts for bulk purchases, please contact
Simon & Schuster Special Sales at 1-866-506-1949 or business@simonandschuster.com.
The Simon & Schuster Speakers Bureau can bring authors to your live event. For more information or to book an event
contact the Simon & Schuster Speakers Bureau at 1-866-248-3049 or visit our website at www.simonspeakers.com.
Designed by Karina Granda
The illustrations for this book were rendered digitally.
The text of this book was set in Neutraface.
Manufactured in China 0217 SCP
2 4 6 8 10 9 7 5 3 1
The book has been cataloged with the Library of Congress.
ISBN 978-1-4814-4952-6 (hc)
ISBN 978-1-4814-4953-3 (eBook)

*To Alyson—*
*may she be showered with*
*sixteen-scoop ice-cream sundaes*
*—T. L.*

**To my darling Shannon,**
**and the ninja inside you**
**—R. W.**

Tonight was the night Joseph would spring into action!
But first he scooted into bed lickety-split, without
panic or protest. This was quite unusual!

His parents congratulated each
other on their superior bedtime
skills. Then they gave him a night-
night peck, tucked him in, and shut
the door.

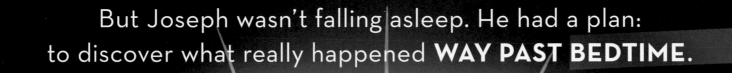

But Joseph wasn't falling asleep. He had a plan:
to discover what really happened **WAY PAST BEDTIME.**

**WAY PAST BEDTIME**, Joseph believed, was when his parents threw the most outrageous parties.

Joseph imagined his parents got gussied up in glittering costumes and hobnobbed with celebrities.

He thought a dozen DJs spun hip-hop hits under spinning neon lights.

Then the partygoers devoured dessert.

*Oh, the desserts!*

Whipped cream and sprinkle pies, colossal doughnuts with cotton-candy centers, and sixteen-scoop ice-cream sundaes. Hot-fudge fountains overflowed!

Joseph longed for a nibble and nosh, but all he had was sour milk. He imagined the full, belly-rubbing guests jostling to view the entertainment.

# Oh, *what a show!*

Fifty Flying Flibbertigibbet
Brothers flipped fantastically. . . .

They were followed by the Astonishing
Allistair, illusionist extraordinaire. . . .

His royal highness Crown Prince Juju judged
a jousting bout and knighted the victor. . . .

Then pirate puppeteers swashbuckled in a perilous performance.

And when the president's top secret ninja task force crashed the shindig, they celebrated with a show of sweet nunchuck skills.

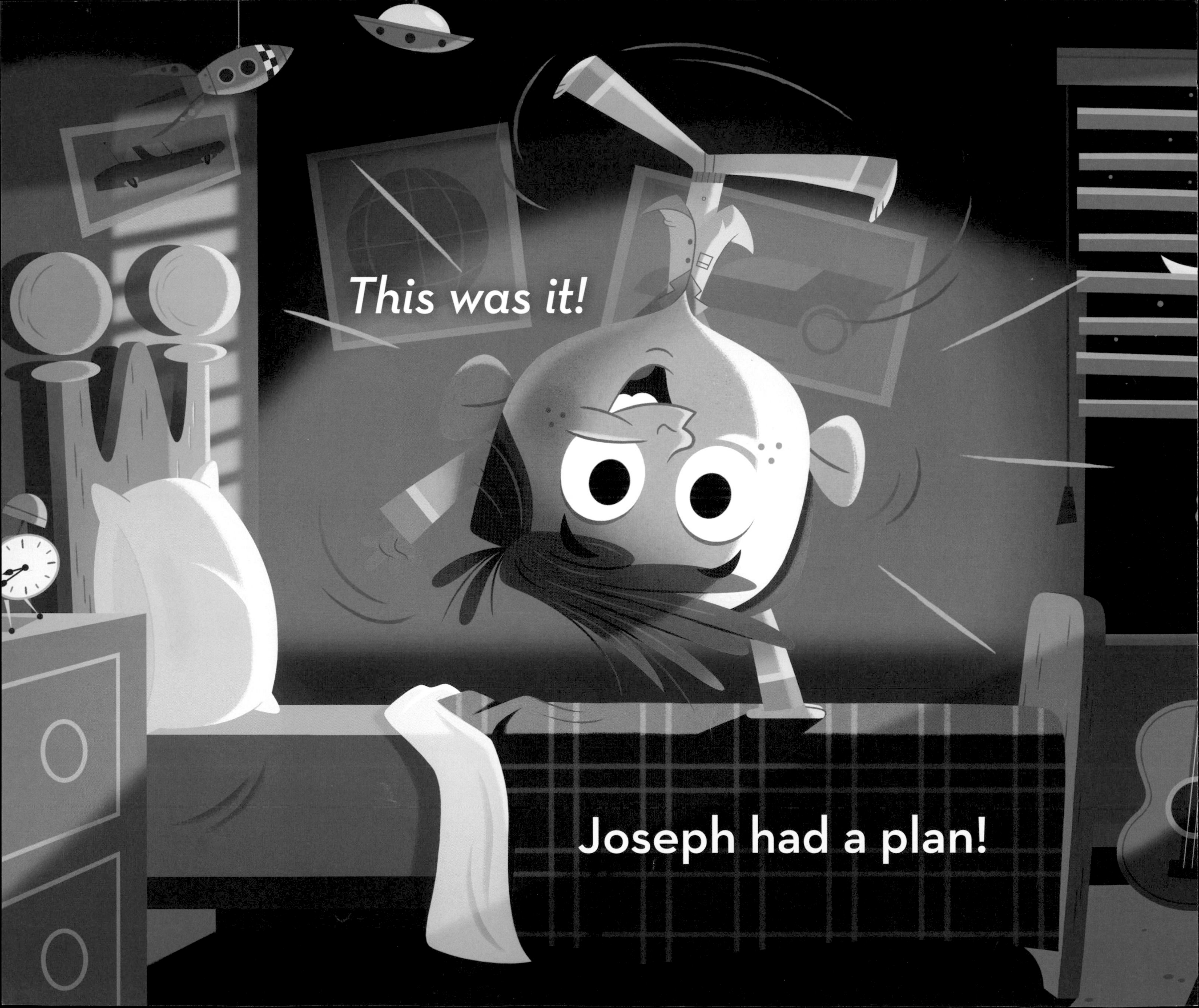

*This was it!*

Joseph had a plan!

He prepared his decoy . . .

instructed the lookout . . .

and tiptoed past the snoozing security guard.

Joseph readied himself for whatever hijinks happened **WAY PAST BEDTIME**.

Joseph slipped under his
invisibility cloak . . .

donned his
night-vision goggles . . .

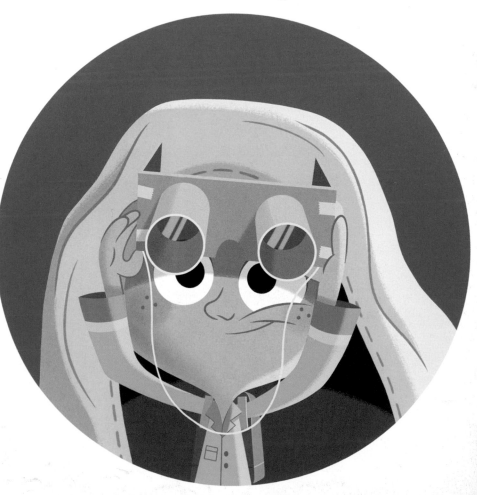

and crept
down
the stairs. . . .

He would learn the secrets of **WAY PAST BEDTIME** and inform his entire school . . . no, the kid population **WORLDWIDE**! They would all demand to be included in the adults' frivolous fun.

Joseph would be a global kid hero!

Joseph waited. He listened. He scribbled notes.
Wait . . . what was *that*?

Had the tuba mariachi marching band arrived?

Or the escaped elephant parade?

It must have been the
juggling lumberjacks!

Joseph slithered under
the stairs and saw . . .

# SNORING?

BORING!

His parents sniffled, snuffled, and snorted awake.

"Joseph, what are you doing up? It's **WAY PAST BEDTIME**!"

"I know why you're sleepy!" Joseph said. "You're tired out from the party."

His parents chuckled. "Party? Don't be silly. Let's all get some rest. It's been a long day."

"This is not fair! This is an outrage!" Joseph protested. But it was no use.

Joseph's parents gave him a night-night peck and tucked him in (tighter this time), and Joseph went to sleep. . . .

... OR DID HE?